Lake Center Elem. School
10011 Portage Road
Portage, MI 49002
269-323-6387

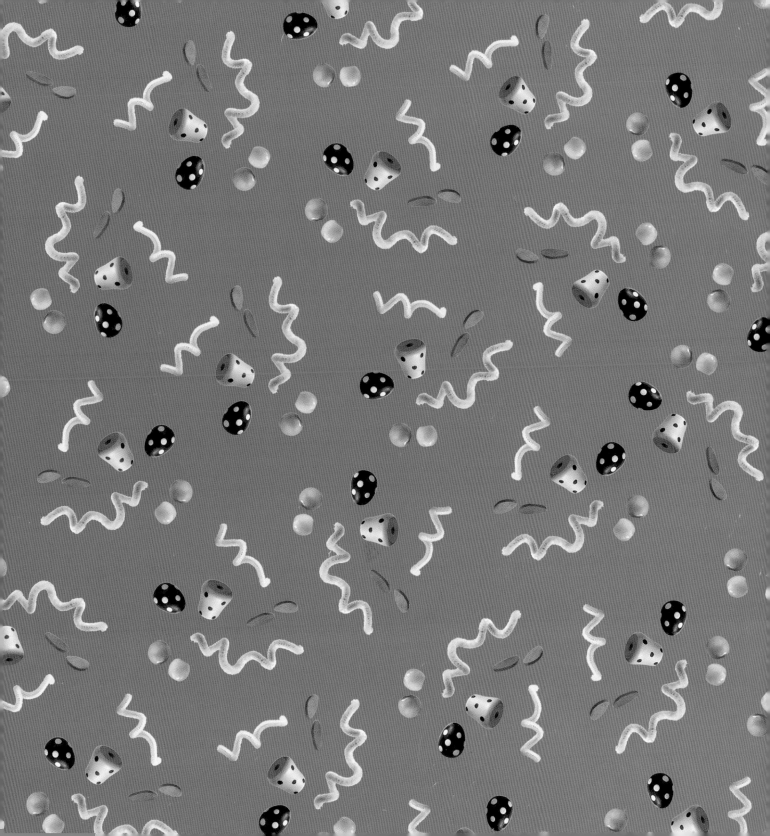

CAN YOU SEE WHAT I SEE?
SEYMOUR
MAKES NEW FRIENDS
A SEARCH-AND-FIND STORYBOOK

WALTER WICK

SCHOLASTIC INC.

New York   Toronto   London   Auckland   Sydney   Mexico City

New Delhi   Hong Kong   Buenos Aires

ISBN 0-439-61780-4

Copyright © 2006 by Walter Wick.

All rights reserved.

Published by Scholastic Inc.

SCHOLASTIC, CARTWHEEL BOOKS, and associated logos are trademarks and/or registered trademarks of Scholastic Inc.

10 9 8 7 6 5 4 3 2 1   6 7 8 9 10/0

Printed in Singapore   46

First printing, February 2006

Acknowledgments

Special thanks to Dan Helt and Kim Wildey for their assistance in the studio; to Michael Lokensgaard for his help with prop making; to Linda Cheverton-Wick for her behind-the-scenes support; to Rich Deas and Stephen Hughes for book design; and to Grace Maccarone for her editorial expertise.

Library of Congress Cataloging-in-Publication Data

Wick, Walter.

Can you see what I see? Seymour makes new friends / Walter Wick.

p. cm.

ISBN 0-439-61780-4 (hardcover)

1. Picture puzzles-Juvenile literature.

I. Title: Seymour makes new friends. II. Title.

GV1507.P47W5135 2006   793.73—dc22

2005010331

TO MY MOM, BETTY WICK

— WW

Can you see a crayon,

3 books, a broom?

Can you
see Seymour

alone in his room?

Can you see
2 spoons,

 a knight, a gnome,

scissors,
and

Seymour leaving
home?

Can you see
a penguin,

a cat,

a chick?

Can you see
Seymour

with a red
craft stick?

 Can you see
a swan,

 a hat made of straw,

 a top, a yo-yo,

 and Seymour's
seesaw?

Can you see
a basket,

3 birds,
a bow tie,

a ladder, and

Seymour way
up high?

Can you see 4 trees,

 a fence that's blue,

2 polka-dot beads,

and Seymour, too?

Can you see
a pipe cleaner,

 2 thumbtacks,

a safety pin,

and Seymour's tracks?

Can you see
 a clothespin,

Clara in a dress,

 a flower,
 a shell,

 Seymour in
 a mess?

Can you see
        a pencil,

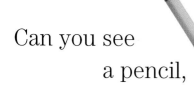

a straw that bends,

a thimble, and

        Seymour...

...with his new friends?

CAN YOU SEE MORE?

In this picture adventure story, written and photographed by Walter Wick, a little toy boy uses pipe cleaners, beads, and paint to make two rabbit friends. You and your child will enjoy helping Seymour find and collect all the things he needs and thinking about the fun all three friends will have in the end. The discussion questions help your child build vocabulary, notice picture details, and more!

Pages 8–9: *Can you see animals—a rabbit, a frog, a bear, and a dinosaur?*

Pages 10–11: *Can you see things to write, color, and paint with?*

Pages 12–13: *What green things can you see?*

Pages 14–15: *Can you see the letter "B"? Can you see the letter "T"? Show me the letter "Y."*

Pages 16–17: *Can you see 1 elephant? Can you see 2 bears? How many marbles can you see?*

Pages 18–19: *How many wheels can you see on the green truck? Do you think the truck has more wheels? Where are they?*

Pages 20–21: *Can you see a blue clothes-pin? Can you see a blue paper clip? What other blue things can you see?*

Pages 22–23: *Seymour is making something. Take a guess. What is it?*

Pages 24–25: *One of the rabbits is made with a red bead with white dots. Can you see that bead in other pictures in this book?*

Pages 26–27: *Seymour and his friends like to ride the seesaw. What do you like to do when you go to the park?*

This book is filled with many things to talk about. Turn this book into a favorite by rereading it, inviting your child to say the rhyming words, or making up new rhymes. You and your child may want to make your very own pipe-cleaner friends.

—Akimi Gibson, Early Childhood Specialist

Walter Wick is the photographer of the I Spy series of books, with more than nine million copies in print. He is author and photographer of *A Drop of Water: A Book of Science and Wonder*, which won the Boston Globe/Horn Book Award for Nonfiction, was named a Notable Children's Book by the American Library Association, and was selected as an Orbis Pictus Honor Book and a CBC/NSTA Outstanding Science Trade Book for Children. *Walter Wick's Optical Tricks*, a book of photographic illusions, was named a Best Illustrated Children's Book by the *New York Times Book Review*, was recognized as a Notable Children's Book by the American Library Association, and received many awards, including a Platinum Award from the Oppenheim Toy Portfolio, a Young Readers Award from *Scientific American*, a *Bulletin* Blue Ribbon, and a Parents' Choice Silver Honor. *Can You See What I See?*, published in 2003, appeared on the *New York Times* Bestseller List for twenty-two weeks. Other books in the *Can You See What I See?* series are *Dream Machine*, *Seymour and the Juice Box Boat*, *Cool Collections*, and *The Night Before Christmas*. Mr. Wick has invented photographic games for *GAMES* magazine and photographed covers for books and magazines, including *Newsweek*, *Discover*, and *Psychology Today*. A graduate of Paier College of Art, Mr. Wick lives with his wife, Linda, in Connecticut.

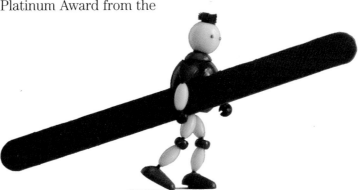

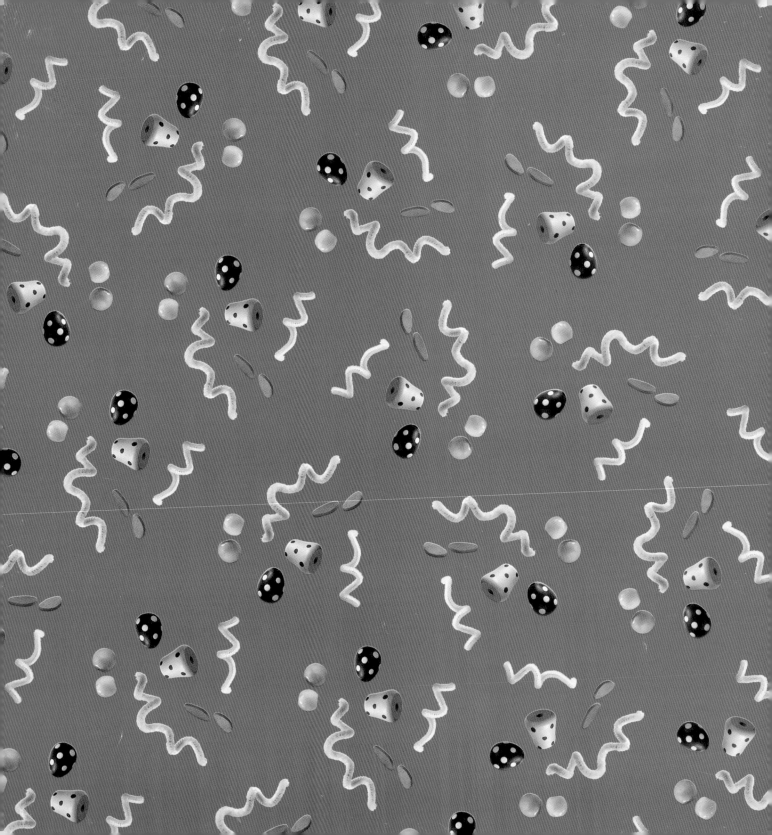